BOOKS BY LAURA (L.A.)MARIANI

Untamed Hearts

The BAD Boy

The BAD Girl

Holiday Romance

14 Days to Love Series: Short Sweet Steamy

Parisian Serendipity

Venetian Whispers

Mumbay Surprise

Romeo in Rome

New York Melody

Artic Embrace

Santorini Sunsets

Havana Heat

Barcelona Dreams

Marrakesh Magic

Vienna Waltz

Sydney Sparks

Amsterdam Affair

Cape Town Safari

Box Set

14 Days to Love: Short Sweet Steamy

Twelve Days of Christmas Series

A Partridge in a Pear Tree: Hot Spicy Christmas Novella

Two Turtle Doves: Hot Spicy Christmas Novella

Three French Hens: Hot Spicy Christmas Novella

Four Calling Birds: Hot Spicy Christmas Novella

Five Golden Rings: Hot Spicy Christmas Novella

Six Geese a-Laying: Hot Spicy Christmas Novella

Seven Swans a-Swimming: Hot Spicy Christmas Novella

Eight Maids a-Milking: Hot Spicy Christmas Novella

Nine Ladies Dancing: Hot Spicy Christmas Novella

Ten Lords a-Leaping: Hot Spicy Christmas Novella

Eleven Pipers Piping: Hot Spicy Christmas Novella

Twelve Drummers Drumming: Hot Spicy Christmas Novella

Box Set

Twelve Days of Christmas

Shadowbrook Paranormal Series

A Halloween Romance: Enchanted in Shadowbrook

The Midnight Hour:A Halloween Shadowbrook Romance

Navy Seals Hunks Series

SEALed Hearts

SEALed with a Kiss

SEALed Undercover

SEALed Pursuit

SEALed Love Code

SEALed beyond Duty

Box Set

Navy SEAL Hunks

A Royal Romance Trilogy

A Coronation Weekend Romance

The Wicked Princess

The Lost Kingdom

Box Set

A Royal Romance Trilogy

The Nine Lives of Gabrielle Series

Gabrielle (prequel/first in series)

For Three She Plays

A New York Adventure

Searching for Goren

Tasting Freedom

For Three She Strays

Paris Toujours Paris

Me Myself and Us

Freedom Over Me

For Three She Stays

London Calling

Back in Your Arms

The Greatest Love

Box Sets

For Three She Plays - Book 1-3

For Three She Strays - Book 4-6

For Three She Stays - Book 7-9

The Nine Lives of Gabrielle Book 1-9 + 3 Bonus stories

Box Set - Italian Edition

Le Nove Vite di Gabrielle: Libri 1-9 + 3 Bonus

ISBN: 978-1-917104-23-4

HER LITTLE SECRET

THE NINE LIVES OF GABRIELLE

LAURA (L.A.) MARIANI

PEOPLE ALCHEMIST

FOREWORD

Her Little Secret is a romance novella for a mature audience - a tale of passion, and the intricate dance between love, betrayal, and forgiveness.

Her Little Secret is a spin-off of the series **The Nine Lives of Gabrielle** and it continues the themes of time, and the effect self-image on our lives.

PREFACE

Time is passing by relentlessly—time past, time present, time future.

But this primary fundamental of physical reality is not what it seems: it's an optical illusion. Physicists tell us that things in the quantum world do not happen in linear steps. They happen now. But you are only aware of the reality you choose to observe.

Consciousness creates the material world—the linear passing of time in stark contrast with the seemingly random crossing of time in our consciousness.

A constant stream of consciousness.

Everything is now—a constant flow connected by some force within each person and memories are a continual connection to events, places, and people and awareness shapes what we experience and choose to see.

Memories, desires, choices—they all exist in the same space, intertwined, linking us to people and moments and a deeper current running through our lives.

The choices made yesterday reverberate in the here and now. The secrets we keep and the desires we hide move through time like shadows, shaping their reality.

" YOUR PAST DOES NOT DEFINE YOU
UNLESS YOU LIVE THERE"
- TONY ROBBINS

GUESS WHAT?

PAOLA

The sun is struggling to break through the thick clouds, casting a faint ray of light across the back garden. The aroma of freshly brewed coffee permeates the kitchen: strong, rich, and familiar. I inhale deeply and savour the moment. I step out onto the patio, and the cool mist dampens my skin. The surrounding trees are shrouded in ghostly white. I wrap my dressing gown tight and sit to gather my thoughts. Martin is still asleep. I love these moments alone before the hustle and bustle of the day begins, lost in my thoughts.

"Come back to bed; I want to be inside you one more time," Marco's ruffled salt and pepper hair caresses his face, tight muscle visible under his tanned skin.

"No, I need to go; I have to get ready, and I have a plane to catch." I rush toward the bathroom and lock the door behind me, "Please, don't follow me," I hope silently. Marco is so masculine; he makes me weak at the knees. The bastard is so arrogant, so secure of himself, I could slap him sometimes. He annoys me so much, his controlling ways. Yet I am so turned on and can't stay away—time after time.

Bang bang!

"Common Paola, common, let me in," he says through the closed door. "You know how much you like my shower trick."

Bang bang!

"Paola, stop being a bitch; I want to fuck you one more time before you go. Open the door; it is an order."

I tremble at the thought of his fingers inside me, and I hate myself for it.

Click.

"That's a good girl. This is what you came for, after all, a good fuck." Marco is standing there, proud of his nakedness, fully erect. He rips my gown open, grabbing my breasts.

"Ouch," the nipples still sore from last night.

· · ·

"On your knees. Now!"

"I am in a rush … I can't …"

"I don't care, on your knees."

Swish—the noise in the kitchen jolts me out of my reveries. I am wet. Damn. Each trip back is heavier and heavier.

Sip, sip.

How did I get into this? Each time, he wants more, more than I can give, and I feel dirtier every time. Yet...

The iPad on the kitchen table buzzes a FaceTime call. Gabrielle from New York. A slender hand with the most humongous diamond and emerald on the ring finger greets me.

"Ciccia, you are going to need some scaffolding on your wrist to carry that. Wow!"

Gabrielle is beaming as she admires the ring. "It's a vintage Tiffany Schlumberger from the Faerber collection. Tom had searched and searched for it since we'd met. He remembered!" a tear coming down her cheek, "Isn't he wonderful?"

"Sorry, did I wake you?" coming back to herself. "Silly me, of course, I woke you up. I couldn't stop myself; I had to tell you."

"Ciccia, you know you can call me anytime. I just made coffee," I reply. "I am so happy for you; you look great."

"What's wrong? You look like shit," Gabrielle says worried.

"Grazie tante, Ciccia!"

"No ... you know what I mean," she continues, "you look like you have been crying."

"You know I don't do tears," I answer quickly. Shit, I didn't realise. "I am just tired, babe. I have just come back from mum's. Probably jet lag!"

"Jet lag from Napoli to London? Behave!"

"Well, maybe I am just getting old," trying to change the subject quickly. I don't want to ruin her moment. "Tell me everything. Will I have to curtsy when I see you next, Viscontessa?"

. . .

"Don't you dare ... I still can't believe it!"

"I am soo happy for you, Ciccia. You deserve it."

"Thank you," she replies. Then she comes closer to the screen, squinting, and looks deeply into my eyes, searching for answers.

"What?" I pause, holding my breath, "I am OK, really."

"We need a good catch-up next week when we return to London."

"Oh, is it 'we' already, uh?"

"No, no, yes ... oh shut up!"

"I am kidding, Ciccia."

"We are getting married in the new year, in Ireland. In his castle. *Incroyable, non*?" She looks so excited, like a kid at Christmas. "You are the maid of honour ... Pardon, matron of honour."

. . .

"I wouldn't miss it." That is so near ...

She adds, "Tom is going to ask Martin to be his best man." Are they that close? "How's Martin?" probing, pressing.

"Asleep," I reply.

"You know what I mean."

"I know. Martin is Martin."

"Babe..."

"I can't wait to see you again next week, Ciccia."

"Me too. See you soon. Bye."

"Bye."

The dull ache in my chest surges as the call with Gabrielle concludes, the weight of my secret pressing down on me with renewed force. I lean against the kitchen counter, my breathing erratic, as memories of time with Marco inundate my mind—our stolen moments in Italy. Marco is so much like my father—larger than life, commanding attention, and oh-so dangerous.

. . .

But it is all a temporary escape from the reality of life. I know that. My eyes drift to my left hand, where a simple gold wedding band mocks me. I remember when I exchanged vows with Martin ten years ago. The man I've married is still there, still the same: the reserved façade, a caring, sweet English gentleman, now a doting husband, father and son. Martin, my one constant in a sea of turmoil.

How have we drifted so far apart? How have I drifted so far?

IT ONLY TAKES ONE YES

PAOLA

The clink of wine glasses and chatter of well-heeled patrons fill Savini, the restaurant once the drawing room of the international belle époque. I settle into my seat, smoothing my pencil skirt. My eyes wander the white-clothed tables until they land on a familiar face—Marco, looking as devastatingly handsome as he did in our university days.

"Paola, che sorpresa!" Marco says, flashing a dazzling smile as he greets me and kisses my cheeks, "Time has stopped for you. Sei Bella come sempre."

"You haven't changed a bit either," I reply, taking in his impeccably tailored suit, salt-and-pepper hair and smooth-tanned skin. Same mischievous twinkle in his eye. "Do you still live in Napoli?"

. . .

"Si, Napoli è casa. Are you still dazzling the business world?" he asks, eyeing my corporate attire. "What brings you to Milan?" he continues, "besides destiny conspiring for us to meet again."

I try to ignore the flutter his words stir in me, but I chuckle like a little girl. "Just a quick work trip. My flight leaves tomorrow morning."

"Perfect, we have time," he says, flashing a dazzling smile. "Come and join me," he indicates at his table.

We catch up over Barolo and un risotto allo zafferano. The years melt away, and the old chemistry crackles between us like electricity. Marco is as charismatic and flirtatious as I remember, his hand now grazing my arm—so different from Martin's cool British reserve.

"I've thought about you over the years, you know," Marco confesses, pinning me with his intense dark eyes. "The one that got away."

That's not how I remember it ... "Marco... I'm married now," and I raise my left hand, the wedding band glinting under the lights of the Galleria. But as I say the words, desire spreads deep in my core. His hand finds my knee under the table, boldly sliding up my thigh.

· · ·

"Cara, what happens in Milan stays in Milan," he reassures me with a cheeky wink. I should stop his hand and pull it away. But God help me, I don't want to. His touch ignites something dormant in me - an illicit thrill, an escape. One night to feel alive again...

And just like that, rational thought deserts me. I open my legs a little. Marco's fingers inch higher, grazing the lace edge of my underwear. I'm breathless, aching, the boredom of my safe, passionless marriage dissolving under his impudent touch. This is so wrong, but it feels so right.

I think of Martin back home in London; when was the last time he looked at me with raw hunger like Marco is now, like he couldn't wait to consume me?

"Don't overthink, Bella," Marco purrs, sensing my hesitation. "Scratch the hitch we never did. This is just a little fun between old friends. Nothing more. No one has to know." His fingers slip past my underwear, boldly stroking me. "Just one time."

Just, just … just …

A moan escapes my lips, my body betraying me. Just one night. A stolen moment out of time. It's not love, just sex - primal, therapeutic, like pressing a reset button. Surely a quick fling couldn't jeopardise everything I've built back home...could it?

• • •

Just ...

Marco settles the bill and rises, pulling me to my feet. "Let's get out of here." His eyes shine with promise, and I'm powerless to resist, even as a twinge of guilt niggles at my conscience.

The air caresses my flushed skin as we exit the restaurant. Marco's arm slung low around my waist, staking his claim. Anticipation and trepidation in my stomach, warring with the pulse of arousal between my legs as he hails a taxi.

What am I doing? Oh God, I can't remember; have I shaved?

No turning back now. As I slide into the backseat beside him, I silence the voice of reason, giving myself over to sensation and sin. For one reckless night, I want to feel something again, even if I hate myself in the morning. The taxi speeds through the lamp-lit streets, a blur of ancient architecture and modern storefronts. Marco's hand rests possessively on my thigh, his thumb drawing maddening circles that make me squirm. I stare out the window, avoiding his penetrating gaze. If I look at him, I'll be lost. But I can feel the weight of his stare, undressing me, setting me on fire.

"Paola." His voice is as seductive as he is. "Look at me."

•　•　•

Exhaling, I turn. His scorching espresso eyes see straight into me, peeling back the layers of propriety. I am starved for passion, aching for it, and he knows it.

"I am going to fuck you so hard," he vows huskily, cupping my cheek. "I'm going to ruin you for your sissy English husband. You are going to come back and beg me for more."

"Don't ...talk ...about ... Mar-t" but I can't continue as his lips touch mine, not quite a kiss, his warm breath mingling with mine—self-preservation and decency battling with raw need.

"Don't speak," he orders. God, he smells good. Crisp and citrusy and achingly familiar - Acqua di Gio. Martin wears the same cologne, but it smells different on Marco. Forbidden. Intoxicating.

I wet my lips, pulse hammering in my throat. "Marco, I-" His fingers sink into my hair as he angles my head and silences me with a deep, long kiss, laying claim to my mouth with lips, teeth and tongue. I moan into the kiss, my treacherous body melting against his, surrendering to his dominance as the taxi flies through the city.

PACKING AND UNPACKING

PAOLA

Time has gone by so quickly. The wedding is this weekend, and we are getting ready to go. I fold Martin's button-down shirt, the soft blue fabric cool beneath my fingers, and carefully place it in his suitcase. The girls' chatter and laughter drift in from down the hall.

"Did you pack the girls' dresses?" Martin asks, his voice even, his eyes fixed on the task.

"Yes, they're in the garment bag." I gesture towards the door, where the bag hangs, the ruffled skirts of the flower girl dresses peeking out.

He nods, a small, tight smile on his lips. "Good. They're so excited."

. . .

"A wedding in a castle in the Irish countryside, with a real Viscount; what little girl wouldn't be thrilled?" I say, trying to match his light tone, but the words feel hollow. I watch him arrange his ties, and I can't help but admire the quiet strength he exudes. I remember the first time we met. I was struck by his subtle, almost elusive handsomeness, which grows more evident the longer you look—the strong jaw, with a certain ruggedness, the English fair complexion that flushes so quickly, and the sandy brown hair neatly trimmed that catches the light as he moves. The glasses perched on his nose lend him an air of refined intellect, but it's his eyes—those steady blue-grey eyes—that truly captivated me. And his reserved, controlled composure from old times gone. The long walks, the endless chats, the courting. I wanted him to kiss me so badly, and I waited. And then I waited some more and waited and waited ... until I couldn't anymore and made the first move.

Not Marco, a philandering scoundrel incapable of showing any affection, a peacock demanding attention, possessive, who fucks me hard, makes me beg and then forgets about me until the next time. And he knows there is always a next time. The stolen moments, the guilt twisting my gut, yet I go back for more, begging.

"This Marco of yours," says Gabrielle, biting into her pappardelle with beef shin ragu, a Trullo's speciality. "He sounds pretty much like your father, *non*?" Gabrielle is the only one who knows my secret."Well, the way you described him anyway ... with your mother," she declares with her typical French directness. Her deep brown eyes staring, searching for a reaction. I don't like where this is going. "You told me you hated your father and your mother for forgiving him each time," she continues.

Oh God, I want the floor to open and swallow me. "Where is the waiter?" I ask, trying to ignore what she said. "We need more wine." I stuff my mouth with a big handful of tagliarini with picked Dorset crab, Amalfi lemon, and chilli, hoping I can stall.

"We do. We need a lot more wine," she presses unperturbed. "Perhaps it will help you to talk about this." When we agreed to meet for lunch at Trullo, a lovely, tiny restaurant just around Highbury Corner on St. Paul's Road, I didn't imagine we would be talking about me.

"Today was supposed to be about you, your big adventure in New York, your reunion, the proposal ... You've just come back, tell me everything!" I say instead.

"Good try. You know the ending," she adds, lifting her left hand and moving her ring finger with the enormous engagement ring.

"I still can't get over how big it is," I say.

Gabrielle smiles like a cat with the cream. "Soo?? Aren't you going to answer?" Still pressing.

. . .

"I didn't hear a question ..." I reply, hoping it goes away.

Gabrielle looks at me pensively and says, "Marco is never going to give you what your father never could."

"Paola ... love?" Martin's voice brings me back to reality, Gabrielle's voice still in my ears.

"Uh?"

"I think that's everything," he says, zipping up one suitcase with a decisive tug. He looks up at me, his expression unreadable. "Are you OK?"

"Yes, yes," I rush to answer. How could I have risked this? This life we've built, this family we've created? I want to say something to bridge the gap that seems to widen with each passing day, but the words stick in my throat. I nod, not trusting my voice. I zip up my case, the sound harsh in the quiet room.

"*La differenza mia cara*, for me it's just sex. I tell Marco I'm going over; if he is available, we meet; if he isn't, it is still OK, like a 'human vibrator' on call. Nothing else. He knows how to make me come, and he does his job. He doesn't want or need anything more from me and me from him". Just sex ... Means nothing ... I can't believe I said that to Gabrielle, like I felt nothing.

• • •

"Girls! Time to go!" Martin calls out, breaking the spell. He grabs both suitcases and heads for the door, his steps measured and sure.

I follow, trying to control my rising emotions. As we step into the hallway, I plaster on a smile, determined to make it through this weekend, one way or another. "Suck it up, Paola," I say to myself, "This is Gabri's and Tom's weekend."

My mind drifts back and forward to the memories I've tried so hard to bury. "Is it true? Am I still looking for his validation?" My father, with his charming smile and wandering eye, always ready with a compliment or a wink for any pretty woman who crossed his path. My mother, silent and stoic, her pain evident in the tightness around her eyes and the set of her jaw. The long nights I'd lie awake, listening to her muffled sobs, waiting for him to come back home from his latest floozy. The mornings after, the heavy silence at the breakfast table, the forced smiles and false cheer. "Is this what I've become?" A woman so desperate for love and validation that I'd risk everything I hold dear?

The drive to the airport is a blur, the chatter of our daughters fading into background noise as I grapple with the weight of my choices. Martin is quiet, absorbed in his thoughts. I want to reach out to him and take his hand in mine, but I can't bring myself to bridge the distance. At the airport, we go through the motions of checking in and shepherding our excited girls through security. They marvel at the planes and bustling crowds, their eyes wide with wonder. I feel a twinge of longing for that innocence. We board the plane and settle into our seats, Martin by the window, me in the middle, and our daughters in the aisle. I feel the weight of my secret pressing down on me. I glance at him, admiring the strong jawline and the silver starting to thread through his sandy hair.

I know my betrayal will shatter him. The thought of losing him, of losing this life we've built together, fills me with terror. The plane takes off. I close my eyes, trying to steady my breathing. "I have to find a way to make things right." I've spent my whole life determined to build a different life, to be different from my mother. "Have I become my father?"

Martin reaches over, his hand finding mine, his touch gentle and reassuring. "Everything alright, love?" he asks, his voice soft, his eyes searching mine.

I force a smile, squeezing his hand. "Just tired," I lie, the words tasting bitter. "It's been a busy week getting ready for the trip."

He nods. "It'll be good to get away for a bit." Martin chuckles a warm, rich sound that usually comforts me but now only amplifies my guilt and shame. He deserves so much better than this. So much better than me. I close my eyes again, trying to block out the thoughts, but they come anyway, unsolicited, unwanted. Flashes of Marco, stolen moments, the thrill, the passion, the aching, the empty aftermath. The plane hums around us, and as I sit here with Martin's hand in mine, and our daughters' laughter in my ears, I feel like I'm on a knife's edge, waiting for the inevitable fall.

LIES, LIES, LIES …

MARTIN

Paola looks at me, clearing her throat. "I think that's everything then. Did you get the car arranged?"

I nod, still not meeting her eyes. "It'll be here at noon."

"Good. Girls, do you have everything packed?" Paola calls out. "We leave for the airport in two hours!" Her dark hair falls in glossy waves around her olive-toned face, eyes flashing with a barely-contained intensity as she glances over. Excited giggles and hurried footsteps sound from down the hall.

"Yes, Ma! Almost done!" Paola smiles.

The girls' exuberance is infectious, even if her enthusiasm feels forced. Silence stretches between us. Paola busies herself with the luggage tags, seemingly unaware of the chasm that has cracked open in our marriage.

"Paola, honey? Your phone is buzzing .... Paola?" She is in the shower, her phone lighting up on the nightstand... I click on the message preview before I can stop and take a peak. My heart pounding.

> "You were a very good girl last night... You were a dirty little slut, you like it when I fuck you hard ..."

The shock is visceral, a gut-wrenching realisation that the woman I love, the mother of my children, has been unfaithful. The name on the screen makes my blood run cold: Marco. The phone clatters from my hand onto the bed, my head spinning, bile rising in my throat. All those trips to Italy, those visits to her sick mother -- how could I have been so blind? The signs were all there. Her distracted air, her renewed passion that felt out of place...

I squeeze my eyes shut against the onslaught of emotions. Sadness, betrayal, and anger crash over me in waves, stealing my breath. How could she do this? To me, to our family? After all these years...

The bathroom door opens, and I hastily replace the phone, arranging my features into a neutral mask. I can't confront her, not now, not with this anger inside, not with the girls nearby. I need time to think and process.

"Martin?" Paola's voice cut through the painful trance. "The car will be here soon. We should get the bags downstairs."

I jolt, swallow hard, and reach for the suitcases. Even now, the wounds are still raw. "Right. I'll take these down." My voice sounds hollow to my own ears. Paola watches me go, her confident exterior cracking for just a moment. Regret flickers across her face, mingled with something akin to longing. But she straightens her shoulders and follows me out, moving in stubborn silence as the distance between us widens.

I still remember every moment and detail of when I first saw her. It was a warm, sun-drenched afternoon in Rome nearly twelve years ago. I was attending a conference in the Eternal City when I spotted her across a crowded piazza. She was laughing with friends, her dark hair cascading in glossy waves, and her olive skin glowing under the sun.

"My God, she's gorgeous," I was transfixed, my heart pounding in a way I'd never experienced before. I just wanted to go over and claim her as mine. I fell hard and fast, desire cursing through my veins, a surge of unbridled possessiveness. It took me nearly an hour to compose myself enough to approach her. I had to control myself. The spectre of my father's abuse and my mother's suffering had left me wary of my own emotions. I feared the intensity of my feelings for Paola, worried I might somehow become the man I despised.

"Paola is having an affair," I blurted out, "Well, regular sex with someone, to be specific ... she is a very passionate woman, " I continued, justifying. "I've never been inclined that way," lies I told myself. "All I ever wanted was a companion and a family. She is an amazing mother and a good wife. We have a great life: she has her career, and I have my family. And I would never leave my girls."

"And you are OK with that?" Tom asked me with a disbelieving look.

"Not exactly, but I have learnt to live with it. She is careful."
    "Learnt to live with it?" more lies. I've shied away from the raw, unbridled desire I crave. That she craves.

"She is a flesh and blood woman with her faults and failures. Flesh and blood, my friend. And you have put her on a pedestal, idolised her. You can't make passionate love to someone you are afraid to break; even I know that". I said that to Tom about Gabrielle. Yes, I- SAID-THAT!

"Have I failed her to be the man she needs? Have I failed me?" The thought lodges like a splinter in my heart. We have built a life together, a family. But the cracks are showing now, the foundation of our marriage straining under the weight of unspoken truths and unfulfilled desires. Mine.

. . .

Paola emerges from the house, our daughters in tow. We begin our journey, the lush English countryside giving way to the promise of Ireland's emerald hills.

"You were a very good girl last night..."

That text plays over and over in my head. "Why didn't I confront her?" I rationalised my decision, telling myself that I couldn't tear our family apart, that our daughters needed both parents and that I could somehow find a way to ignore it and move forward. I watch Paola settle into the passenger seat beside me. The thought gnaws at me as the Uber drives through the countryside. The silence between us is thick.

Tom's and Gabrielle's love story plays out in his mind...

"Man, this is crazy. You can't go to New York and wait at the top of the Empire State Building without knowing if she will show up. I know New York is home for you, but still, it's crazy," I said. "It has been six months without contact."

"Have you told Paola you know about her and her Italian stud?" Tom replied.

My cheeks went red. "Touché."

. . .

"Gabrielle has everything she needs if she wants to come over and see me: plane ticket, hotel reservation. She just needs to be sure she still wants it. She still wants me, us".

His gamble paid off.

I glance at Paola, taking in the elegant lines of her profile. She is still the most beautiful woman I've ever seen, she makes my heart race and my soul ache. As we arrive at the airport, I brace myself for the journey ahead.

"This weekend belongs to Tom and Gabrielle." Viscount Thomas Darcy Vitale Fitzwilliam II, actually, "My problem can wait until Monday."

The road ahead would be difficult, a battle, but I am finally ready to wage it, no matter the cost.

ROSINGS PARK
PAOLA

The stately manor house rises before us, a limestone Georgian beauty nestled amongst emerald green hills that roll endlessly to the horizon. Tom's ancestral estate, recently inherited after the truth of his noble lineage came to light. I take it all in—the ornate wrought iron gate, the manicured hedges lining the gravel drive, the marble fountain tinkling melodically in the courtyard. It's like stepping into the pages of an Austen novel—breathtaking, romantic, idyllic—everything Gabrielle deserves for her wedding.

"Welcome to Rosings Park," Tom greets us with a broad smile, one arm wrapped around Gabrielle's waist. She looks radiant, at home in her new role as lady of the manor.

Martin reaches for my hand as we ascend the limestone steps, but I slip mine free to hug Gabrielle instead, pasting on a smile. "It's gorgeous, Gabri. It's like a fairy tale! I'm so happy for you." My words sound brittle to my own ears. I avoid Martin's eyes.

. . .

I inhale deeply, the fresh and clean air tinged with the scent of salt off the nearby sea. Tom clasps Martin's shoulder, his grin wide and welcoming. "Martin, Paola! Let me introduce you to the family."

He guides us into a grand foyer, all marble and gilt, where a small gathering awaits. Tom's brothers, as tall and striking as he is, flank an elegant elderly woman in a velvet armchair. Gabrielle's parents are nearby, her mother's curious gaze sweeping over me.

"Everyone, this is Paola, Gabrielle's friend, her husband Martin, and their lovely girls, Sofia and Emilia." The girls smile shyly, overwhelmed by the opulent surroundings.

"Ah, Paola!" Tom's grandmother rises, taking my hands in her papery grip. "I've heard so much about you. And what a handsome couple you two make!"

If only she knew …

"Thank you, Lady Fitzwilliam. We're delighted to be here," I murmur.

Gabrielle's mother approaches, air-kissing my cheeks in the French fashion. "Paola, *comment vas-tu chérie?*" Her eyes, a piercing dark brown so like Gabrielle's, seem to penetrate my very soul.

"Très bien, Madame." The pleasantries slip out naturally, even as my stomach twists with anxiety. I love Madame Arkin. Her gaze lingers on my face a beat too long, her lips pursing. She senses something amiss between Martin and me, but discretion prevents her from prying. For now.

"Come, let me show you to your rooms," Gabrielle interjects, rescuing me. "You must be exhausted from the trip."

Gratefully, I follow her up the sweeping staircase while Martin and the girls go wandering. As the door closes , I sink onto the plush four-poster bed, my head spinning. The opulent surroundings fade away as my mind churns. A soft knock at the door startles me. "Paola? Are you decent?" Gabrielle's voice, muffled by the heavy oak, is laced with concern.

"Come in," I call, straightening my shoulders and pasting on a smile.

She enters, her dark hair tumbling around her shoulders. "Is everything alright, *chérie*? You seemed... tense earlier."

"I'm fine, just tired from the journey."

· · ·

Gabrielle studies me, her head tilted. "Paola … Did you two have a fight?"

My smile falters, and I look away, blinking back sudden tears. "No, no. I'm fine …. don't worry about me. This is your weekend."

She moves closer, resting a comforting hand on my arm. "*Chérie*, you'll get through it. You and Martin, you're meant to be together. Anyone can see that."

I nod, swallowing hard. "Thanks, Gabri." I hug her fiercely, drawing strength from her.

A chime sounds from somewhere within the house, signalling the start of the festivities. "That'll be the dressing gong," Gabrielle says, pulling back. "Mum's insisting on a formal dinner tonight to welcome everyone. Will you be alright?"

"Of course." I square my shoulders, determined to play my part. "Let me freshen up, and I'll be down shortly."

———

I take a deep breath, trying to steady my nerves as I make my way down the grand staircase. The sound of laughter and chatter drifts up from below, and I pause for a moment, my hand gripping the polished railing. Martin is waiting at the bottom, looking dashing in his tailored suit. But there's a distance in his eyes that wasn't there before, a coolness that sends a shiver down my spine. He offers me his arm, and I take it, forcing a smile.

"You look beautiful," he murmurs, but the words feel hollow.

"Thank you." I smooth down the silk of my dress, feeling the weight of every eye in the room upon us as we enter the dining hall.

The table is set with gleaming silver and crystal, and the centrepieces are a riot of colourful blooms. Tom's grandmother, the Dowager Viscountess, presides at the head, her keen gaze missing nothing. "Paola, my dear," she says, beckoning me closer. "Come, sit by me."

I obey, grateful for the reprieve from Martin's presence.

Across the table, Gabrielle's mother catches my eye, her brow furrowed in concern. "Is everything alright, *chérie*?" she asks softly, her French accent lending a musical lilt to the words.

I force a bright smile, hoping it reaches my eyes. "Of course, Madame Arkin. Just a bit tired from the journey, that's all."

• • •

She looks unconvinced but lets the matter drop, turning to speak with her husband. I pick at my food.

The evening stretches on forever, each course more lavish than the last. By the time the plates are cleared, and the men retire to the library for brandy and cigars, I'm exhausted, my cheeks aching from the effort of maintaining a facade of cheerful serenity.

I make my excuses and slip away, seeking the solace of our bedroom. Martin chatting away with Tom and his brothers. The girl are in their room. I sink onto the edge of the bed, my head in my hands, and finally let the tears come, hot and bitter, against my skin.

I KNOW

MARTIN

The phone lights up in the dark with an incoming message. Paola moans and stretches, slowly pulling herself up from the bed.

Buz, buzzzz.

She reaches out and then stops. "Go on, take it," I say, "Take it," Paola looks terrified.

"Here," and I drop the phone on the bed, "Read it. ... Don't you want to know what your lover is doing?"

"What do you mean?"

"There's no point pretending anymore," my voice is wavering but eerily calm. "I know what you have done."

The words are coming out, and I can't stop them. "Every time you went to Italy, I knew." My heart pounds against my ribcage. The room spins slightly, and I reach for a hand to steady myself.

"Martin, I..." Her voice cracks.

"Don't you dare deny it," I step closer, my jaw hurting. "Do you have any idea how much it killed me inside, Paola? Wondering what you were doing with him? The images torturing my mind? And you just went on lying to my face."

Tears spill down her cheeks. "I'm so sorry. I never meant to hurt you."

"Well, you did hurt me—you pulled me apart." My voice rises, echoing off the ancient walls, my hands balled into fists at my sides, my broad shoulders shaking.

She reaches out slowly to touch my arm, but for the first time, I flinch away as if burned. "Don't!" I warn through gritted teeth. "I'm trying so hard not to lose control right now ..."

I can't turn into Him. I won't.

• • •

"You're nothing like him," she whispers as if knowing. But the words sound hollow. Gabrielle and Tom's laughter drifts up from the courtyard below.

"Tell me how to fix this," she pleads. "I'll do anything. I love you, Martin."

Tears stream down my face, the anger finally gushing out. The stone walls seem to close in around us. The truth is finally out. She knows I know.

"Martin, I..." her voice cracks, the words catching in her throat. "Please, let me explain. It was a mistake, a terrible mistake. I was weak."

I can't believe she said that. "A mistake? You call months of lying and sneaking around a mistake?" My jaw clenches some more.

"I know I don't deserve your forgiveness, but I'm begging you, Martin. Please don't give up on us. I love you, and I'll do whatever it takes to make this right. " Her words are too much to bear. Doesn't she know?

"Give up on you? WTF, Paola!" the pain is now intolerable, "I fucking LOVE you! I fucking meant those vows ... For better, for worse ... in sickness and in health ... till death do us part. Those vows ... those vows were not just pretty words on a pretty day." My voice is strained, "I stood there and promised, knowing change will happen and still commit to being together ... till death DO US PART."

Paola's head snaps up, her eyes filled with disbelief and hope. "You love me, even after what I've done? Why didn't you say anything?"

"Why didn't I say anything? Why?" why didn't I? "Because I was waiting for you to stop. Because I wanted you to choose me, to want me, us, more." I move closer. "You are fucking mine, you belong to me." She is still wearing her tight red dress. I pull the straps down and grab her large breasts, squeezing her nipples. "These are mine!"

She looks at me then, really looks at me, and a long moan escapes her lips. I pull and squeeze some more before turning her over. I lift her dress and place my hand between her soft thighs, pulling at her lace underwear. "This pussy is mine."

"Martin," she quivers.

I back her down against the bed, pinning her with my body. I can smell her arousal over the faint scent of her perfume. I groan in her ear, "You're mine, Paola. Mine, do you hear me?"

"Yes, ..."

       . . .

Her lace black undies are soaked, and I rip them off before sliding my fingers into her wet heat. "Oh, Martin," she moans, her back arching, her hips pressing against me. I press a finger into her slippery opening, then another, circling my thumb over her swollen clit, making her whimper and squirm under my touch. Her hands grip the edges of the bed, screaming.

"Do you like being claimed?" Her response is a loud cry, and I know she does. Anger replaced by an overwhelming desire to pound into her.

"No, no, please don't stop," she whines as I pull my fingers out.

"I'm going to fuck you all night," I growl, and I thrust deep into her, over and over. "Whose pussy is this?"

"Yours, y-ooou-rs ..."

My hands roam up and down her body, cupping and squeezing her breasts. I can feel myself nearing the edge.

"Come for me, baby." She screams my name over and over as I continue to pounce into her tightness, feeling it pulsing and tightening around me. Finally, she falls over the edge, and I let myself go too. I should have done this a long time ago.

THE BIG DAY
PAOLA

The morning light seeps through the thick curtains, casting a warm glow on the tangled sheets. Martin's arms are still wrapped tightly around me, his grip soothing and protective. I nestle deeper into his embrace, not wanting to leave this safe haven.

"Good morning," he whispers, softly kissing my hair.

I turn to face him, taking in his handsome face. The man I've always desired has been here all along, by my side. "Thank you," I whisper back, a smile spreading across my lips.

"Well, I was good," he chuckles, waggling his eyebrows mischievously. "Fucking awesome, actually..." We both burst into laughter. "I can always do a repeat performance now if you'd like." His voice is low and suggestive, his hardness pressed against me.

. . .

"I'd love to," I reply breathlessly, my desire growing at his touch. "But we have to get ready for the big day. The girls will be knocking down the door any minute now."

Martin groans playfully, knowing that our duties call for us to rise now and start preparing. "Yes, the flower girls are beyond excited for their role. And their pretty flowy dresses." He grins, picturing our daughters' excitement and enthusiasm for the upcoming event. We reluctantly untangle ourselves from each other and start getting ready for the day ahead.

The bedroom door opens, "Mum, Dad," Emilia and Sofia burst in, their voices loud and full of excitement. Martin and I erupt into laughter, glad we stopped when we did.

"I'll jump in the shower first and then go to help Tom to get ready; I'll take my suit with me."

I nod. "I'll see you later."

"We'll meet at the altar again, Mrs Rossi-Wright," he says.

"Mrs Wright," I reply and nods smiling.

———

The grandiose estate is adorned with swaths of white silk and arrangements of fragrant blossoms, all ready for the wedding. The scent of jasmine and gardenias hangs heavy in the air, mingling with the delicious aromas wafting from the adjacent feasting hall. The sun glows over the manicured gardens, bathing the scene in a warm, ethereal light. The guests are all adorned in their finest attire, fit for the occasion.

Sofia and Emilia walk down the aisle, gently tossing rose petals. "They look so happy, I am so proud". Gabrielle walks behind them on her father's arm, wearing a breathtaking ivory gown with lace appliqués and a sweeping train. I can see her eyes sparkle as she sees Tom waiting for her at the altar, looking tall and handsome in his tuxedo. I stand by Gabrielle's side as her matron of honour while Martin is beside Tom as his best man, looking ever so dapper in his suit.

The scent of fresh flowers fills the air. The family chaplain begins the ceremony, his voice steady and warm. As Tom begins reciting his vows first, I catch Martin's eye and see him silently mouthing the words along with Tom. My own throat tightens: "In sickness and in health...for richer and for poor...till death do us part."

I can feel tears filling up my eyes. I can't cry, I can't cry ...

As Gabrielle takes her turn, I move my lips along with her: "In sickness and in health...for richer and for poor...till death do us part."

. . .

After the ceremony, the wedding party moves to the sumptuous feast on long banquet tables adorned with silverware and crystal glasses. Servants circulate the room, refilling glasses with the finest wines and liquors. After the meal, the orchestra plays a lively waltz as the newlyweds dance their first dance, followed by the traditional father-daughter dance.

"Mrs Wright, may I have this dance?"

"With pleasure, Mr Wright."

Martin leads me on the dance floor, his hands firm on my body, pulling me close, claiming me once more, gently kissing my forehead. I sigh into the kiss, my arms wrapping around his neck like I fear he'd disappear. Martin's hand trails up and down my hips while he kisses down my jawline, his tongue flicking my sensitive spot.

"Martin," I moan, my nails digging into his back.

He breathes against my skin, "I love you, Paola," his voice deep with emotion and desire.

"I love you too, Martin." With that, he claims my lips. The room is filled with laughter and heavy breathing, but the most important sound of all is the sound of our hearts now beating in sync.

EPILOGUE

D ing dong ... Ding dong ... Ding ...Dong.

Sunlight streams through the vibrant stained glass windows, radiating a kaleidoscope of colours across the Church's ancient stone walls. Gabrielle and Tom are beaming with pride as they cradle their precious bundle, their faces shining with the love and wonder of new parenthood. The Church is full, and the soft murmur of loved ones gathered to celebrate the occasion fills the air.

Martin leans close to my ear and whispers, "It will be us ... soon." His hand finds the slight swell of my belly, a secret we've yet to share with the world. I glance at Martin, taking in the confident set of his shoulders and squeeze his hand, my heart full of love and gratitude. My man. My husband.

. . .

The priest begins the ceremony. Gabrielle and Tom approach the baptismal font with their newborn daughter in their arms.

He then calls us forward, "Paola, Martin, Are you ready to help the parents of this child in their duty as Christian parents?" Snif snif. Gabri's mother is sobbing with joy.

"We do," we answer in unison, our voices strong and clear.

"Is it your will that Anne Shobhan Vitale Fitzwilliam should be baptised in the faith of the Church, which we have all professed with you? "

"It is."

"Anne Shobhan, I baptise you in the name of the Father," He says, pouring water on her forehead, "and of the Son," pouring water upon her a second time, "and of the Holy Spirit."

As we exit the Church, Martin pulls me close, his lips brushing against my temple, his hand possessively firm on my back. I tilt my face up to his and return the kiss. A boyish grin spreads across his face. "How are you feeling, love?" he murmurs, his breath warm against my ear, and pulls me into his strong embrace, his hand resting protectively on the gentle swell of my belly. I feel a rush of desire.

· · ·

"Perfect," I whisper back, leaning into his touch. "Absolutely perfect."

QUOTE

" MARRIAGE IS THE SCHOOL OF LOVE WHERE CHANGE IS
INEVITABLE. YOU CAN CHOOSE WHETHER YOU GROW TOGETHER
OR APART."

\- FR . MIKE SCHMITZ
(SUNDAY HOMILY 29 OCTOBER 2021)

AFTERWORD

Self-image is our self-limiting portable box. It is a hidden force that shapes our relationships, desires, and even betrayals—it defines the limits of the world we create.

We constantly adjust to its confines like thermostats, and when we step too far from our comfort zone, we return to familiar paradigms. Sometimes, in the pursuit of fulfilment, we betray not only others but also ourselves.

Are we really searching for what we want or illusions that keep us from true intimacy? Do we seek perfect lovers and perfect lives while avoiding the very vulnerability required for love to flourish?

Constantly chasing what we could have or whom we might meet means we ignore what exists all around us that already IS incredible. Or, even worse, the wonderful people who are all around us.

Happiness and fulfilment already exist and it starts with us. First and foremost. One day at the time.

GET YOUR FREE EBOOK

Sign up the Laura (L.A.) Mariani mailing list for a FREE steamy romance.

You'll be the first to hear about new releases, exclusive offers, bonus content and all Laura's news. You can even email her back. She loves chatting with her readers!

To claim your free ebook visit:
https://laura-mariani-author.ck.page/freeshortstory

AUTHOR'S NOTE

Thank you so much for reading **Her Little Secret**.

I hope you enjoyed the story. A review would be much appreciated as it helps other readers discover the story. Or a few stars perhaps - the more the better ;-) !

Thanks.

Laura xx

Places in the book

I set the story between real places in London and New York and fictional places in Ireland.

You can see some of the places/mentions in the story below - find out more about them or perhaps, go and visit:

London

- Highbury & Islington
- Trullo.

New York

- Empire State Building

Milan

- Galleria Vittorio Emanuele II
- Savini

Bibliography

I read different books as part of my research. Some of them together with other references include:

A Theory of Human Motivation - **Abraham Maslow**
Catholic Rites of Baptism - **Diocese of Westminster**
Psycho-Cybernetics - **Maxwell Maltz**
Self Mastery Through Conscious Autosuggestion - **Émile Coué**
The Artist Way - **Julia Cameron**.
The Complete Reader - **Neville Goddard**, compiled and edited by **David Allen**
Tools of Titans - **Tim Ferris**

ABOUT THE AUTHOR

Laura Alexandra (L.A.) Mariani is a best selling author of Short & Steamy Romance | Where Alpha Males Meet Fierce Heroines for Sweet Endings, your go-to author for captivating romance tales that will sweep you off your feet and keep you on the edge of your seat!

When Laura is not weaving stories of love, desire and suspense, you'll find her exploring the vibrant streets of London, drawing inspiration from its hidden corners and bustling markets, or strolling through the charming streets of Paris, savoring street food in Rome, or relaxing on a sun-kissed beach in Bali, her journeys fuelling her creativity and infuse her stories with wanderlust.

You can also follow her on